The Little Golden Book of
Jokes and Riddles

By Peggy Brown
Illustrated by David Sheldon

A GOLDEN BOOK • NEW YORK

Text copyright © 2013 by Peggy Brown
Illustrations copyright © 2013 by David Sheldon
All rights reserved. Published in the United States by Golden Books, an imprint of
Random House Children's Books, a division of Random House, Inc., 1745 Broadway, New York,
NY 10019. Golden Books, A Golden Book, A Little Golden Book, the G colophon, and
the distinctive gold spine are registered trademarks of Random House, Inc.
randomhouse.com/kids
Educators and librarians, for a variety of teaching tools, visit us at RHTeachersLibrarians.com
Library of Congress Control Number: 2012931232
ISBN: 978-0-307-97916-2
Printed in the United States of America
10 9 8 7 6

It's About Time!

Why did the girl throw the clock out the window?
To see time fly!

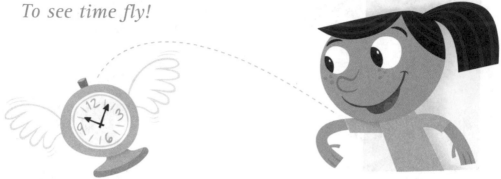

What time is it when you need to see a dentist?
Tooth-hurty.

When does a golfer need an extra pair of socks?
When he gets a hole in one!

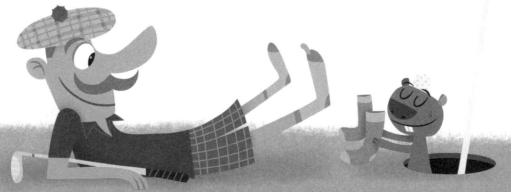

What time is it when a flying saucer full of Martians falls out of the sky, crashes through the roof, and lands on your lunch box?
Time to get a new lunch box.

Knock, Knock!

Knock, knock!
Who's there?
Olive.
Olive who?
Olive YOU!

Knock, knock!
Who's there?
Ken.
Ken who?
Ken I come in the door, or
should I climb in the window?

Knock, knock!
Who's there?
Window.
Window who?
Window you think you'll finally open the door?

Knock, knock!
Who's there?
Yuck.
Yuck who?
Yuck-an have these cookies back—they're awful!

Knock, knock!
Who's there?
Banana.
Banana who?
Knock, knock!
Who's there?
Banana.
Banana who?
Knock, knock!
Who's there?
Orange.
Orange who?
Orange you glad I didn't say "banana" again?

Elephunnies!

How do you stop an elephant from charging?
Take away his credit cards.

What was the elephant doing at the baggage claim?
Waiting for his trunk.

How do you make an elephant float?
*Two scoops of ice cream, lots of root beer,
and one elephant.*

Mom: Don't be selfish, Mike. Let your sister have the sled half the time.

Mike: She does, Mom. She has it going up the hill and I have it going down!

Tom: More cake, please!

Mom: Tom! If you eat any more cake, you'll burst.

Tom: Pass the cake and get out of the way!

Oink Yoinkers!

What do you call a pig in a pointy hat that flies over the beach on her broomstick?
A ham sand witch.

What do you call a pig that's not sharing the mud with others?
A ground hog.

GO AWAY!

MINE

What do you call an itty-bitty pig?
Hamlet.
What do you call it when Hamlet cuts firewood?
Pork chops.
What do you call it when Hamlet steps on an apple while chopping firewood?
Pork chops and applesauce.
What should you call if Hamlet hurts himself while chopping wood?
A hambulance!

This Little Pig . . .

This little pig went to the airport.
Hamlet was his name.
He headed for Chicago
For a Ping-Pong tournament game.
He boarded the plane very proudly,
And a tiny tear formed in his eye.
Hamlet knew he was making history . . .
On the day that a pig could fly.

The Chicken and the Egg

Why did the chicken cross the road?
To get to the other side.

What days do chickens hate the most?
Fry-days!

Why did the chicken join the band?
He already had the drumsticks!

What kind of marks did Sheldon the egg
get on his report card?
Egg-shell-ent!

What tickles a chicken better than feathers?
A yolk book!

What do you call a mud-covered chicken
that crosses the road and then crosses back?
A dirty double-crosser.

If you're an egg scrambling down the
freeway, where should you get off?
At the neggst eggsit.

Mary: I just laughed so hard at those chicken jokes that I swallowed a chicken bone!
Dad: Are you choking?
Mary: No, I'm serious!

Johnny: I found a monkey!
Katie: You should take him to the zoo!
Johnny: I took him to the zoo yesterday, and we had so much fun that I'm taking him bowling today!

LANE 2

Mom: Riley! Did you take a bath?
Riley: No. Why, is one missing?

Mom: Come in and help me fix dinner.
Riley: Why, is it broken?

Riley: Mom, can I have a TV dinner?
Mom: Sure. Would you like your TV boiled or roasted with gravy?

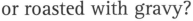

Jack: I walked in front of a car, and guess what happened?
Grampa: You got tired!
Jack: Then I walked behind the car, and guess what happened next?
Grampa: You got exhausted!

Prehistoric Jokes!

Why did the dinosaur cross the road?
He liked chicken.

What do you get when two dinosaurs
crash into each other?
Tyrannosaurus wrecks!

What's the only vegetable that will be left in your garden after a dinosaur walks through it?
Squash.

What do you get if you cross a triceratops with a kangaroo?
A tricera-hops!

Jeff: I keep seeing apatosauruses with orange polka dots.
Jane: Have you seen an eye doctor yet?
Jeff: No, just apatosauruses with orange polka dots.

Purrfectly Funny!

What happened to the
mama cat that swallowed
a ball of yarn?
She had mittens.

What do cats eat for breakfast?
Mice Krispies.

If I'm holding five cats in one hand
and nine kittens in the other, what
do I have?
Really big hands.

What wild cat is no fun
to play games with?
A cheetah!

Riddles in Black-and-White!

What's black and white and blue?
A sad zebra.

What's black and white and quickly turns gray?
A skunk rolling down a mountain.

What's black and white and whistles?
A referee.

What did the judge say when the skunk walked into the courtroom?
"Odor in the court!"

"You're pretty dirty, aren't you, dear?"
"Yes, and I'm even prettier clean!"

"Waiter, what's this fly doing in my soup?"
"The backstroke."

Mom: Sally, how could you get your feet so wet when you were wearing your rain boots?
Sally: It was pretty hard, but I did it!

Did you hear about the fight in the candy store?
A lollipop got licked.

And there was another one over at the bakery shop.
Two buns got fresh.

Spooky and Kooky!

Why couldn't the skeleton cross the road?
He didn't have the guts!

What do mummies like to eat for dessert?
I scream.

What do goblins drink when they're thirsty?
Ghoul-ade.

Where do yetis go to dance?
To snow balls.

What did one yeti say to the other?
"I'm afraid I just don't believe in people."

What can you get from a vampire in wintertime?
Frostbite.

I've Got a Million of 'Em. . . .

Why did Cinderella get kicked off
the basketball team?
She ran from the ball.

"Waiter, this coffee tastes like mud!"
*"Well, sir, it was ground this morning
and we added water."*

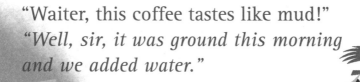

Why can't pirates play cards?
*They're always standing
on the deck.*

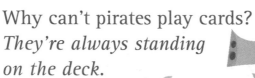

What did the big firecracker say to the little firecracker?
"My pop is bigger than your pop."

What did the big rose say to the little rose?
"Hiya, bud!"

There was trouble over at the railroad station this morning—a ticket got punched.

How Do You Say Goodbye . . .

. . . to a German apple dessert?
"Toodle-oodle, Apple Strudel!"

. . . to a bowl of spaghetti?
"Toodles, Noodles!"

. . . to a curly-haired dog?
"Poodle-oo!"

. . . to a french fry?
"Later, Potater!"